**BLUE MOUSE PLUS
PLUS PLUS PLUS PLUS
PLUS PLUS PLUS**

WRITTEN BY:

DREW A LOT

WILL WRIGHT

HUGH MANN HUMAN

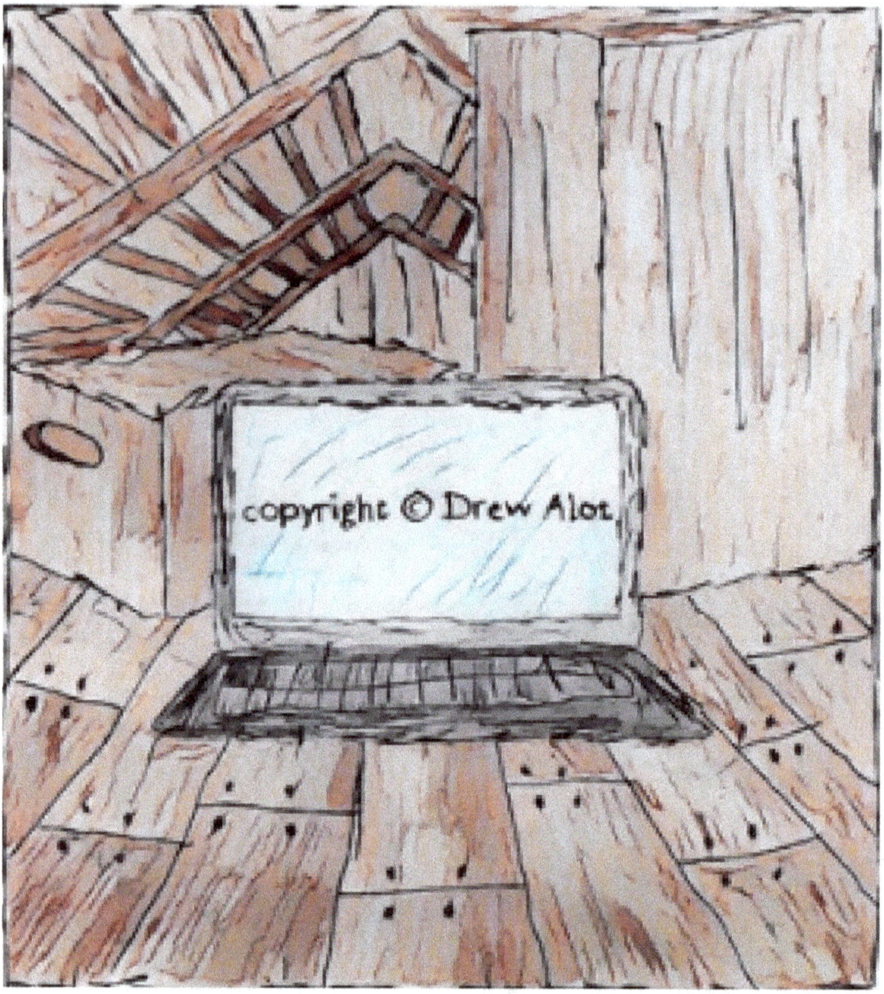
copyright © Drew Alot

Date Published:

ISBN:

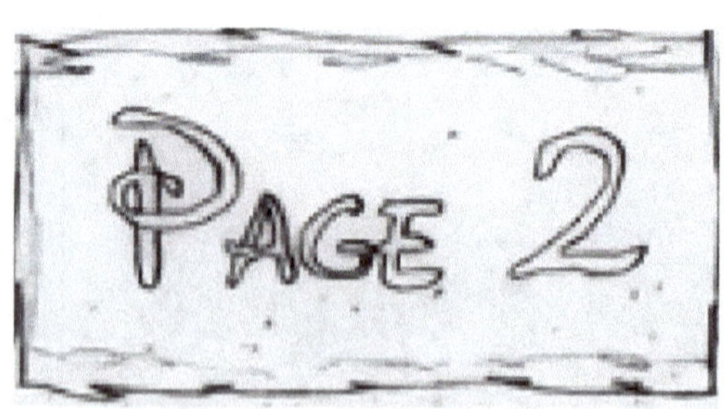

PAGE 2

CHAPTER 1 – ZOMBIE APOCALYPSE

But that's when she saw
someone crawling on the path.

Tall thin 24-year-old Alexander was sobbing softly. All she could really see what his thick-brown-wavey hair as his head was still down....

He crawled and crawled to the wooden steps of the porch.

He climbed up the steps and looked up at Debbie.

His big
dark brown eyes had tears in them.

She saw his reaction and cried

He put his head back down! Debbie imagined that something serious must have happened!

She quickly and carefully got down to his level and put her hands on his shoulders.
She was growing curious yet

scared. All she could do was ask him.

Her soft brown eyes looked him in the wide brown watery eyes.
With confidence she softly asked

He just continued to sob.....

She looked behind her and then around for help but no one else was here. She looked at him and asked

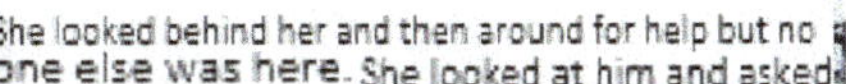

He sobbed

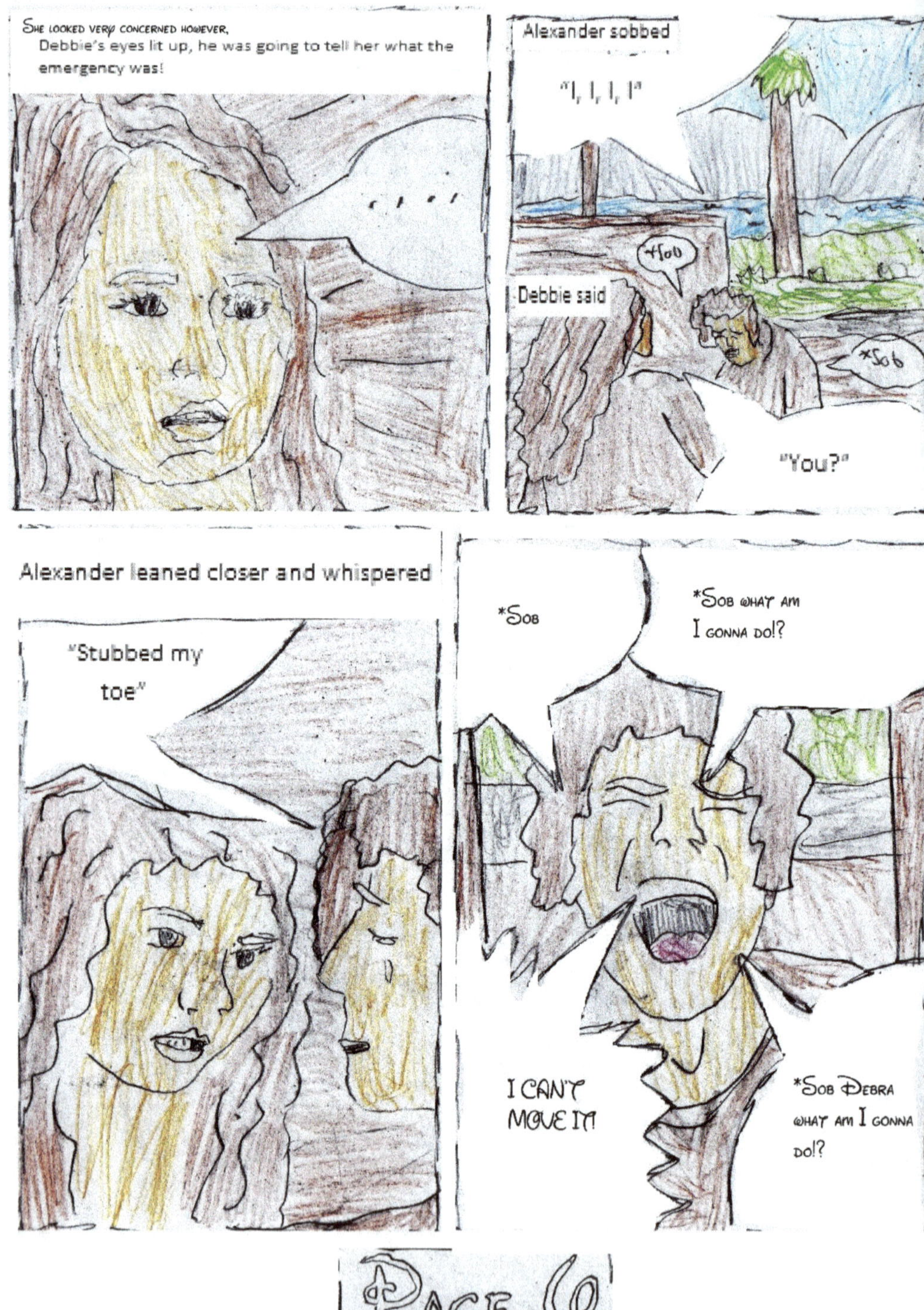
She looked very concerned however,
Debbie's eyes lit up, he was going to tell her what the emergency was!
Alexander sobbed
"I, I, I, I"
Debbie said
You
"You?"
*Sob
Alexander leaned closer and whispered
"Stubbed my toe"
*Sob
*Sob what am I gonna do!?
I CAN'T MOVE IT
*Sob Debra what am I gonna do!?
PAGE 6

There was a silence.....
....
Debbie's jaw was dropped.

She slowly nodded her head,
....

and took her arms off his shoulders.   She then sniggered.
*Snigger
!?

Page 7

Alexander cried.
Debbie stood up and put her hand out to help him up.

She sarcastically teased...

As he took her hand and stood up. She softly explained

"It's not the end of the world"

Suddenly!

An air raid siren blasted and echoed from all speakers throughout the state of California!

THREE CHARACTERS FROM THE FIRST DRAFT (SERENA, NOAH AND BARRY) WERE HIDING IN THEIR HOUSE IN THE LA SUBURBS

This chilling dystopian-like alarm only meant one thing!

It's the end of the world!

WHO CARES ABOUT THE FANCY PAGE NUMBERS

Alexander cried

"WHAT IS THAT!? WHAT IS THAT THING!?"

Debbie looked around in awe and said "Ugh! That's the A.R.C Siren!"

She hastily turned,

picked up her phone and listened.

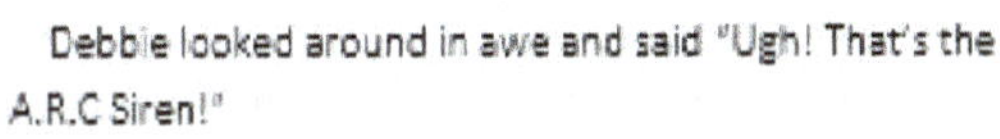

An automated echoed warning sounded from the speakers. A deep British masculine voice was heard saying "ALERT! ALERT! THIS AN AUTOMATED MESSAGE FROM THE A.R.C"

"A Zombie virus has swept the streets once again, all citizens that have not been affected are to stay inside and turn all lights off until further notice from the A.R.C."

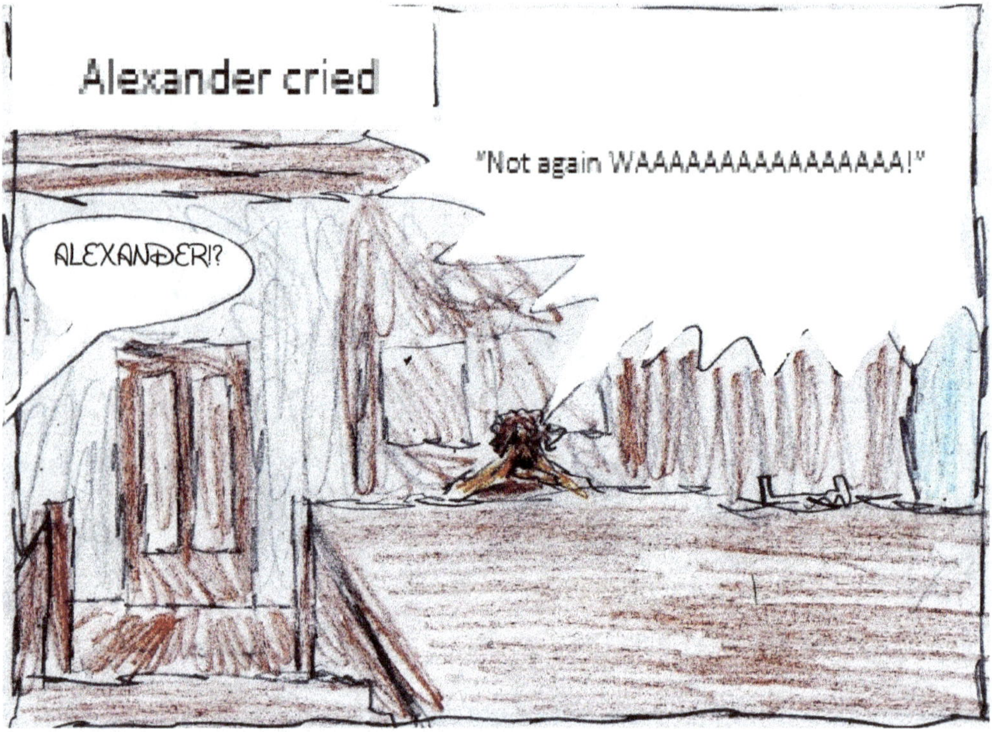

Alexander cried

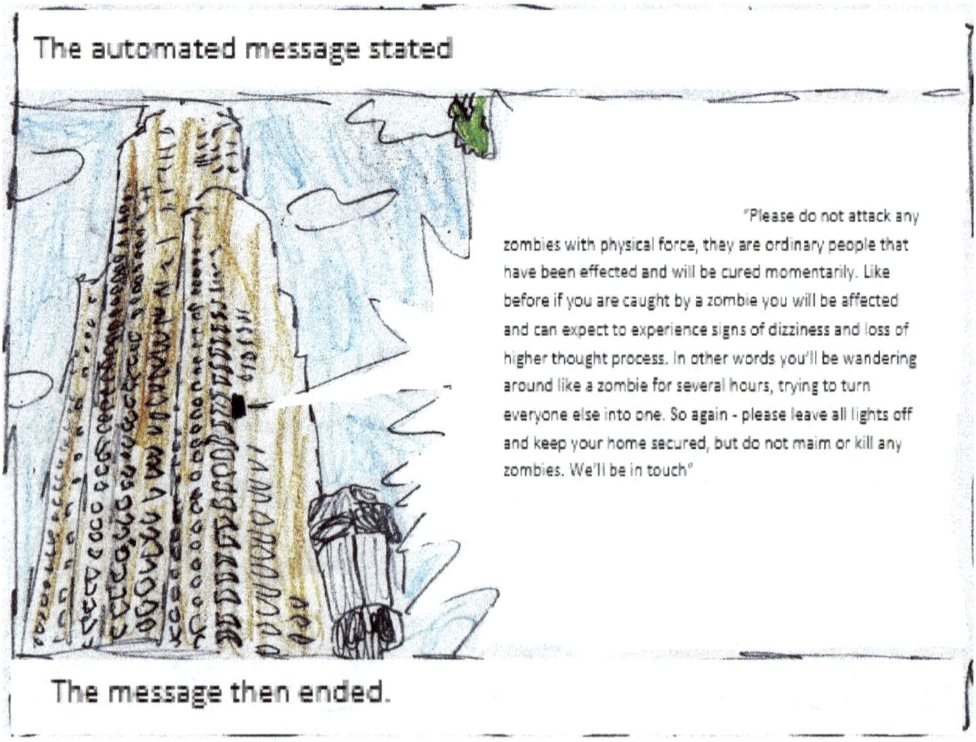

The automated message stated

The message then ended.

Meanwhile in L.A.

Pale-eyed and Dazey-looking Zombies were limping and reaching their arms out as they wandered and groaned. They filled the streets! They had even made it to the suburban areas!!!!

BANG! BANG! Some zombies were banging on the doors of the large luxurious houses

while other Zombies were trying to swim in the pools!

With haste! Debbie and Alexander opened the front door! They got inside!

Debbie looked around! Their large luxurious home had too many points of entry!

First of all she shut the big finely furnished door!

She then started pushing the sofa it scraped the floor as she did. Alexander came to help!

Alexander cried "Real nice! Reeeeeeal nice! How does this happen without the A.R.C noticing!? HOW DOES THIS HAPPEN WITHOUT THE A.R.C NOTICING!?"

Debbie dropped her arms for a break. She softly explained "I-I don't know but, look the A.R.C will cure ALL the zombies, they did it before"

There was a silence as she promised "They'll do it again, right?" she felt like she was telling herself this as well...

Alexander sighed as they then continued heaving the sofa.

The sofa was now pushed in place by the big brown double doors.

Alexander stood up tall and put on a smug serious face.

He stated "Let us be thankful the zombies are not trying to eat our brains" Debbie nodded saying "Exactly"

He bragged "Even if they were I wouldn't be scared because, I, am not scared of anything"

TO BE CONTINUED

www.ingramcontent.com/pod-product-compliance
Lightning Source LLC
Chambersburg PA
CBHW060806210726
48292CB00013B/1904